EXCITING
TITLES FROM

MW01124027

Contemporary Fiction & Sports Adventures

TALES OF THE UNCOOL
6-Book Series

These are the stories of the nerds, geeks, and freaks of Halsey Middle School — and how six self-proclaimed 'uncool' tweens took over their school.

Grades: 4-6
Ages: 8-12   Paperbacks: $8.99
Pages: 64   Library Bound: $27.99

MAGIC LOCKER ADVENTURES
6-Book Series

Three young friends find a magic locker, which takes them back in time. Historic sporting events are in jeopardy unless they right history!

Grades: 3-5
Ages: 8-11   Paperbacks: $8.99
Pages: 48   Library Bound: $27.99

ON THE HARDWOOD 30-Book Series

MVP Books invites readers to stand alongside their favorite NBA superstars *On the Hardwood*. These officially licensed NBA team bios provide an exciting opportunity to learn about where a team has been, and where they are going...

Grades: 4-6
Ages: 8-12   Paperbacks: $8.99
Pages: 48   Library Bound: $27.99

Common Core Aligned   twitter.com/bookbuddymedia   facebook.com/bookbuddymedia

ORDER NOW!

Contact Lerner Publisher Services:
www.LernerBooks.com
Call: 800-328-4929 • **Fax:** 800-332-1132

Lerner
PUBLISHER SERVICES

N.J. CORBO

Last Line of Defense
Heads or Tails

Scobre Educational
2255 Calle Clara
La Jolla, CA 92037

Scobre Operations & Administration
42982 Osgood Road
Fremont, CA 94539

www.scobre.com
info@scobre.com

Scobre Educational publications may be purchased for educational, business, or sales promotional use.

Cover and layout design by Jana Ramsay
Copyedited by Renae Reed

ISBN: 978-1-62920-254-9 (Soft Cover)
ISBN: 978-1-62920-253-2 (Library Bound)
ISBN: 978-1-62920-252-5 (eBook)

A Heads or Tails *Adventure*
in Middle School Basketball

Scobre Educational

HOW TO READ THIS BOOK

You should start a *Heads or Tails* book like any other, on page 1. At the bottom of each page, you'll see a direction to move on to the next page, *or* you'll be presented with a choice: *Heads or Tails?*

Heads   Tails

Flip a coin (or just pick randomly), and turn to either the "heads" page or the "tails" page to continue the story. Or, you can read more about each option, and choose the path that sounds the best to you.

You can read this book over and over and never take the same path twice. Enjoy your journey into the glory, and agony of middle school basketball!

Chesterton Middle School Dragons – Key Players

Phil "Fixer" Halverson, Center, 8th Grade

That's YOU! Your defensive skills are so amazing, they call you "Fixer," because if the offense is not pulling their weight, they can always rely on you to set things right by blocking lay-ups and dunks, and jumping on rebounds. You can't make a free throw overhand to save your life, but your underhand toss is pretty good. Too bad you never show anyone.

Tommy Gildea, Point Guard, 8th Grade

He's the shortest on the team, but also the quickest. His handles and driving are pretty good. He is lethal once he gets to the paint, because he's fast and can spin back and forth to get off an open shot. He's a mad scorer. He's not necessarily a powerful defense, since he goes for so many steals, but he's a decent passer, though more likely he'll be looking to score first.

Matty Gildea, Shooting Guard, 8th Grade

He has agility and strength, and can play down low or anywhere. He can drive both ways decently. He has speed and good decision-making skills, and he's an okay shooter. His handles are solid as well, but not great. His passing skills are excellent.

Ashton Green, Small Forward, 7th Grade

He's your most explosive player and can get up really high for a rebound. He's strong and can defend well. Good handles, great at dribbling and passing.

Mark Cunningham, Center – 2nd string, 7th Grade

About four inches shorter than you and decently athletic, he has pretty good handles. He drives and finishes to his left, but isn't as good on the right. He's a solid shooter and a very energetic defender. He's the guy who goes in when Coach subs you.

Late fall means bonfires, pumpkin muffins, big piles of red and orange leaves, and, best of all, basketball season. It's usually your favorite time of year.

You are Phil "Fixer" Halverson, center for the Chesterton Middle School Dragons. You're tall for 13 (six-one, to be exact), and you're fast. You may not be able to make an overhand free throw to save your life, but on the court, you're in control – at least, you used to be. A lot of things have been changing recently.

Before a big game, your mom normally makes hotdogs and cookies decorated like basketballs. She cheers and yells out the Dragon's rally cry: "Dragons, dragons everywhere. You can run, but you can't hide, from dragon fire and dragon pride!" Tonight though, she barely opened a plastic container of cheese puffs, and now she's just staring at them like they offended her. She looks like she might cry.

You gently take them from her and force a smile. "I'll get it, mom."

You wish your mom wasn't sad, but you try not to think about it. The big game against the Lindonville Lions is in two days, which means it's time to get pumped. It seems like Lindonville and Chesterton have been racing each other for first place since the beginning of time. The towns compete over everything from holiday decorations to environmental friendliness, and forget about sports. It's crazy. Even though people get more excited about the high school teams, you guys still feel the pressure.

Luckily, some things haven't changed. So, as usual, your best

Go on to the next page.

friends are over. Tommy and Matty, the twins you've been friends with since kindergarten, and Ashton, who you met last summer, when he moved in near your grandparents. It was at a game of pick-up in the park. Although you only have two inches on him, he couldn't get the ball by you. No one could. That day, Ashton gave you the nickname "Fixer" because when things were going south for your team's offense, you just kept fixing it on the defense.

You're all sitting on the rug in your living room. Matty is flipping through offensive plays in the playbook.

"What's up with your mom?" Tommy asks, as you toss him the cheese puffs.

"I dunno. She's been weird lately." You say, and quickly change the subject. "We need to go over some defense too, Matt."

"Why, dude? We've got you," he laughs.

Tommy tells Matt to open his mouth wide, so he can shoot cheese puffs into it. He makes six in a row and you all cheer.

Still crunching, Matty says, "Alright, Fixer, what do you do in Press Breaker if you're playing five and three has the ball?"

"Hang back in case they reverse it," you say. But then your brain kicks in and you correct yourself. "No, I mean, run down the court."

Your face feels hot. You should know that. What's going on?

"C'mon, Fixer," Ashton teases, "gets yer head in the game, son."

You try to laugh it off, but you know your head isn't in the game. You feel like your grandparent's dog, Pepi, whenever you say, "Let's

Go on to the next page.

go, boy" – confused and a little worried. At least you do okay with the rest of the plays.

After the guys leave, your little brother, Jesse, emerges from his dark hole of a bedroom and sits by the fireplace with his tablet. He's swiping at the screen madly, probably playing some dumb video game where he cuts or crushes things. You don't like those. You like destroying zombies. There's just something great about saving the world. You walk over and sit on the couch.

"Hey, Jess, did you finish your homework?"

"Shut up, jerk, you're not mom," he scowls, and then adds, "Where is mom, anyway?"

"I think she's in her room. I'm gonna make a PB&J. You want one?"

"Fine," he sighs.

It's late when your dad gets home. You hear your parents' bedroom door slam and your mom stomps down the stairs. You hate it when they fight. It makes your chest and throat feel tight, like something is pressing down on you, and then your head starts to hurt.

Well after midnight, the house is silent, but you're still staring at the glow-in-the-dark stars on your ceiling, wishing you could make the pain in your head stop. Next thing you know, it's morning. The garage door opens and the Petersons' dog barks as your dad drives away.

You bolt out of bed and bang on Jesse's door.

"Get up, bus'll be here in 15."

Downstairs, there's no sign of your mom, so you throw a couple

Go on to the next page.

frozen waffles in the toaster. While they cook, you splash water on your face, get dressed, and grab your backpack.

Jesse still isn't up.

"Dude, c'mon!" you yell into his room, and he tumbles to the floor in confusion.

"Not cool, Phil," he hisses.

"Just get ready," you plead, knowing that there's little chance you'll make the bus at this point.

Back downstairs, you put some peanut butter on your waffles and throw two more in the toaster for Jesse. He comes stumbling into the kitchen. Looks like he got even less sleep than you.

"Where's your backpack?" you ask.

"Ugh," he grunts and goes back upstairs.

When you get out the door, the bus is halfway down the block.

Even though you run the seven blocks to school, you're still late, which is really not good. Coach is a stickler for rules, and believes academics come before sports. You avoid him all day but, as you're heading into the locker room before practice, he stops you.

"Listen, Halverson," he says – Coach never calls you "Fixer." "You've been distracted lately, and now today you're late for school. What's going on?"

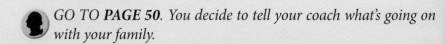

GO TO **PAGE 50**. *You decide to tell your coach what's going on with your family.*

GO TO **PAGE 26**. *You assure him everything is fine and it won't happen again.*

Listening to your dad yell at Jesse makes you feel sick to your stomach, but you don't know what to do, so you put your headphones on and start your English homework. After a while, the yelling stops and there's a knock on your door. It opens slowly. Your dad doesn't look as big as usual. In fact, he looks like someone let the air out of him. His shoulders are bent, and his eyes seem sunken back in his head. He looks like a deflated version of himself.

He doesn't say anything. He just picks up a picture from your dresser. It's of the two of you playing hoops in the driveway. Your dad never says "basketball." He says "hoops." You always loved that. He taught you how to play, and he's been so proud of you, but it seems like he just doesn't have time for you anymore.

He's standing there, shrunken, staring at the picture, and you can feel yourself getting angry. You've always thought of him as the strongest guy around. Indestructible. For some reason, the way he seems right now, it's like he's broken a promise.

"Dad," you say, ending the silence. "I think you were too hard on Jesse. If you weren't gone so much, he probably wouldn't get in so much trouble."

"Phil, you're talking about things that you do not understand," he says, regaining some of his height.

"You're right. I don't understand," you say. "Nothing makes sense." Before he has a chance to respond, you tell him to just forget it and flop onto your bed, rubbing next to your eyes. That stupid headache

Go on to the next page.

is back.

Just as you're finishing up math, there's another knock. This time it's Jesse.

"Hey," he says, leaning against the door frame. "I just wanted to, uh," he hesitates. "I just wanted to say thanks."

"For what?"

"You stuck up for me with dad."

"Oh, yeah, right" you say. You hadn't actually considered that that's what you were doing. You just wanted your dad to know he was messing things up for everyone.

Jesse looks out into the hall, but doesn't move to leave.

"Do you remember our fort?" he asks without looking at you.

"Sure, it's still in Grandma and Papa's backyard. Why?"

"That was cool," he says.

You and Jesse used to do a lot of cool things together. You built forts, captured salamanders; you even used to play hoops together.

"Yeah," you agree, and then ask, "So, what were you thinking trying to steal liquor?"

"I dunno," he says and kicks the door frame. "Justin dared me and I figured I could get away with it. Nobody's ever paying attention."

You realize he's right and want to do something about it. Part of you wants to take him and go play some ball right now, but you'd have to sneak out. Then again, you could just invite him to your next practice.

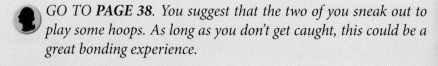

GO TO **PAGE 38**. *You suggest that the two of you sneak out to play some hoops. As long as you don't get caught, this could be a great bonding experience.*

GO TO **PAGE 10**. *You don't want to risk getting Jesse in more trouble, so you invite him to your basketball practice.*

You're a little freaked out about seeing a counselor, but you agree to go. Everything with your family is just too much to handle on your own.

"Good choice, Phil." Coach slaps you on the back. "Now let's go practice, and get ready to fry some Lions."

The next day, you go with Coach to the counselor during your free period. You're surprised how easy it is to talk once you start, and you feel a surge of openness every time Coach nods. The counselor talks about taking care of yourself, but you're not sure what that means yet. Still, something heavy has been lifted off you – you can breathe again.

Your focus is back on the game and it's not a minute too soon. As the starting center, you get the tip-off. You're a good leaper anyway, but today you feel like you might just touch the sky. Tommy's a strong post player, so he lines up on the offensive end of the circle. He's your mark. Matt and Ashton line up on opposite sides of the circle at the half-court line.

The ref blows his whistle and the ball is up. You leap, tip it to Tommy. He pivots, redirects to Ashton. Matty blocks out the Lions' defense, and Ashton goes in for the breakaway lay-up. It's in and you're off to a great start.

Tonight, their offense doesn't stand a chance against the Dragons and Fixer Halverson. The Lions' Ricky Jensen goes for a shot. You're right behind him. You leap when he does and slam the ball away from the net. You guys are on fire, and you roast the Lions: 30 to 19.

Go on to the next page.

After the game, you see your mom and Jesse, and your dad is with them. They're all smiling, and your mom gives you a double thumbs-up.

Outside, your dad's leaning against his car, waiting for you.

"You played a great game tonight," he says.

"I didn't think you'd make it," you say.

"Yeah," he says. "I didn't know if I would, but your coach called me." He pauses and takes a deep breath, and you wonder what Coach told him. "You're a really strong defender," he finally says.

He puts a hand on your shoulder.

"On the court, you're the last line of defense," he says, "but you should just get to be a kid at home." He looks sad and happy at the same time, and you're not sure what to say. That's when he hugs you.

You don't know what's going to happen next, but you know things are finally changing.

THE END

Why did it have to come down to you and a free throw? You can't knock down an overhand free throw. You've tried. As you jog to the top of the paint, it occurs to you that there is a way out of this altogether. You could play up your injury.

You grab your shoulder and head toward Coach. Your stomach feels hollowed out, like someone reached in and grabbed all your guts. You really don't want to fake an injury, but you also don't want to be the reason your team loses.

Coach looks at you hard, like he's X-raying you.

"Whadda ya think, Halverson, can you make the shot?"

You're thinking, *C'mon, you know I can't,* but, "I don't think so," is all you say.

"Is it the shoulder?" he asks. "It's really giving you some trouble, huh?"

His words are meant to be supportive, but they sting instead. Each word pokes at you like a bully when he's calling you names: wimp, liar, fake.

"Yeah, it hurts," you say through clenched teeth. You look down in frustration, filled with anger and confusion about what to do.

"I don't want you to push it, Halverson," Coach says. "It's up to you."

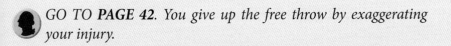

GO TO **PAGE 42.** *You give up the free throw by exaggerating your injury.*

GO TO **PAGE 35.** *You've never done it successfully before, but Coach believes in you, and he just wants you to try. You attempt an overhand free throw.*

You don't want Jesse to feel like nobody's paying attention to him. When you were 10, your dad taught you how to shoot, pass, and block. You realize Jesse hasn't had that same kind of time with him, and you want to help make up for it. Even though you'd really like to head out to the court right now, and play some one-on-one to get your minds off things, you think it would probably be better to avoid getting Jesse in more trouble, so you're trying to figure out how to invite him to hang with you.

"You know," you say, with a little hesitation. "If you wanted to do something fun after school, you could come to practice with me."

"And do what?" he wants to know. "Sit there like an idiot, watching you guys?"

"No, no. Of course not," you assure him. "You could do stuff with us. Practice, I mean."

"Why do you, all of a sudden, want me to hang out with you?"

"I dunno," you say. "I guess you kind of reminded me that we used to have a lot of fun together."

He's skeptical at first but, somehow, you talk him into it, and you're feeling pretty proud of yourself too. The next day, instead of hanging out with his kleptomaniac friends, he's going to come to the gym and it's all because of you.

After school, you look for Jesse outside the gym, but he's not there. You make a few laps around the gym, in case he went to the wrong door, but he's nowhere to be found. You can't believe it. You totally

Go on to the next page.

thought you'd talked him into it, but maybe he was only saying what he thought you wanted to hear.

Just when you're about to give up, you hear some boys talking behind the football bleachers and you recognize Jesse's voice. It sounds like he's trying to leave, but the other boys keep talking to him.

"Yeah, but that was so messed up," one boy says. You think it's Cal from the way he lisps.

"Totally," another boy chimes in – probably Justin. "I can't believe that guy called your mom."

"At least he didn't call the cops," you hear Jesse say, and the other two laugh. You can tell that Jesse isn't joking though.

"Here, have a smoke, Jess," you hear Cal offer.

You run around the side to where you can see them and call over to Jesse. He looks at you somewhat desperately, like he's been waiting for you to show up. His face almost says: *where the heck have you been?*

You're completely relieved.

"C'mon, dude, we'll be late," you say, trying to sound annoyed so the guys won't give him a hard time for leaving with you.

"Sorry, guys," he says. "I'll see ya," and he runs over to you.

Coach is like a mind-reader; he invites Jesse to join in on drills before you even have a chance to ask. You're doing a body balance drill called "Red Light, Green Light" today. It's kind of like the game you used to play when you were younger, and you know Jesse remembers it too.

Go on to the next page.

"Alright, guys," Coach says. "Keep your knees bent, hips back, and shoulders over your feet. And keep your shooting foot forward whenever I say 'stop.'"

He has you line up in front of him and tells you to be quick, but don't hurry. He says it's all about learning to be in control.

A lot of things are still out of control right now, but on the court, you are back in control . . . and you're happy. You want Jesse to have something like that too. As you run drills, talking and laughing with your friends, you look over and see him smiling. Maybe you can't fix everything, but this seems like a good start.

THE END

Ellie wants to know about any weekend pick-up games, but you're afraid the guys won't be into a girl joining your Saturday game. You can't lie to her, but you try to downplay it.

"Um, yeah, ya know, sometimes we shoot hoops at the rec center."

Ellie stops walking and turns to you.

"My big brother taught me how to play," she says. "We used to play all the time. But then he left for the Navy." She tucks her hands in her pockets and looks away. "He's been away two years, and I really miss him. Now I mostly just practice by myself." She turns back to you. "I really love playing basketball," she adds.

Ellie looks at the ground for a moment and then at you. You're still not sure if this is a good idea, but she's looking at you with those big green eyes of hers, and you can tell that she really wants to play basketball. A girl who loves basketball as much as you do – how cool is that? Besides, you know how much you'd hate it if you couldn't play, except for in gym class.

"I suppose you could come . . . " you start to say.

"That would be awesome!" She practically screams before you can finish your invitation.

"I think I can talk the guys into letting you play one game," you add quickly, before she gets her hopes too high. She doesn't care. She gets the biggest smile on her face and starts jumping up and down. She gets some pretty good air too.

Go on to the next page.

"I really appreciate this, Phil. I promise, you won't regret it."

As soon as you bring it up to the guys though, you do regret it.

It's Friday night and you're at Tommy and Matty's house, downstairs in their basement. Their dad turned it into a playroom, with carpet, recliner chairs, and a huge TV for movies and video games. They also have tons of board games and a really elaborate track for racing cars. They have more than a thousand cars too. You're holding a little red sports car, spinning the wheels, not making eye contact with any of them.

"Dude, a girl?" Ashton says, and smacks his forehead with his hand.

"I dunno, Fixer," Tommy adds. "I mean, have you even seen her play?"

"Yeah," you lie. "She's alright." They don't seem convinced.

"Look," Matty says in a mock-serious voice. "We all know you've got the hots for her, but why does she have to play basketball with us?"

Tomorrow you'll be going to the rec center to play, so if you're going to convince them, you need to do it now.

"C'mon guys, it'll just be for one lousy game," you plead.

"Wait. Did you already tell her she could play?" Ashton asks.

"Kinda," you admit.

Just then, Ashton gets a funny look on his face. His eyes narrow and his lips curl into a devious smile. He tosses the Nerf ball and

Go on to the next page.

makes the shot.

"What will you give us?"

"Huh?"

"What will you give us if we let Ellie play?"

"Aww, man," you say. "What do you want, Ash?"

You know he's always had his eye on your Clippers jersey, and that's exactly what he wants. You tell him it's not a fair trade, and you're going to remember the next time he wants something, but he doesn't care. He loves that jersey.

"Do you guys want stuff too?" you ask Matty and Tommy.

They don't, but they say you owe them.

You wake up feeling weird. But today, it has nothing to do with your family. You're not sure if it's because you're nervous about how badly Ellie's going to play, and so how bad the guys are going to make fun of you for it, or if it's because you're nervous to see her. Either way, the eggs your mom offers you are not going anywhere near your mouth. You grab a piece of toast instead and head out the door.

It's a chilly walk to the rec center, but the sun is shining. When you walk in, the guys are practicing their shots. Ellie walks in right behind you.

"Hey, Phil."

"Hey, Ellie."

You chuckle awkwardly, not knowing what else to say. Luckily,

Go on to the next page.

you don't have to think for long, because Tommy comes jogging over.

"So, we usually play two-on-two," he says, "but I'll sit out for Ellie's game."

Is he flirting with her or just being a good buddy? Who knows? But you decide not to worry about it. Your mind is plenty occupied with the game at hand.

You all take a few practice shots and Ellie misses the first two, but then nails the third. You think maybe there's some hope. It's you and her against Matty and Ashton, so Tommy tosses the coin. First possession goes to you and Ellie. You're a little worried she'll be timid, but it's immediately clear that she's definitely not afraid. Ellie fronts Matt for you and slips behind him. You instinctually pass her the ball and move toward the basket. She spins and tosses the ball around Ashton. You get it, fake a pass, and go for a jump shot. It's in – a perfect pick and roll, and you've never even played with her before. It's a match made in heaven.

Now Matty has the ball, but not for long. He dribbles and takes a few steps toward the net, but Ellie snatches the ball and tosses it to you behind her back. You hear Tommy say "Dang!" in the background, and you're thinking the same thing. This girl's got skills. You shoot from the wing and make it.

"Hey," Tommy teases Matty, "you want me to wring you out? Cuz that girl is mopping the court with you."

Go on to the next page.

"Ha-ha, very funny," Matt says back.

Ashton grabs your arm and leans in to whisper something to you.

"Listen," he says "you can keep the jersey if I can have Ellie on my team next week."

You laugh and tell him you'll think about it. This is going to be interesting.

THE END

You can't keep covering for Jesse; no matter what you do, it doesn't seem to help. Jesse tries to shove the smokes into his backpack, but Mrs. Doyle already saw them.

"Cigarettes, young man?" she asks disapprovingly.

For a moment, you think he might deny it. But, sounding defeated, he says, "Yeah."

"Give them to me," she demands. "You're going to Mr. Diggle's office, and we're calling your parents."

You wince, knowing that Jesse is in for it this time. Your grandpa on your mom's side died of lung cancer, and both your parents think smoking is one of the worst things a person can do to their body.

"Great," Jesse says under his breath.

"I'll come with you," you say. You still feel protective. He says you don't need to, but you go anyway.

The principal's office is a large room with windows all around it. He's always watching, but once you're inside, you feel like everyone is watching you – you're on display, like a fish in a bowl. Mr. Diggle starts lecturing your brother about smoking. He wants to know if he thinks it looks cool. He tells Jesse that he should be more like you – an athlete who gets good grades – and that's when Jesse loses it.

"Not everyone can be perfect like Phil," he yells. Jesse has been yelling a lot lately. He never used to be so angry, but the worse things get with your parents, the worse he behaves. You wish the principal hadn't compared you.

GO TO PAGE 39.

Ellie is looking for a weekend pick-up game, but you don't want her to ask if she can play with you and the guys. They won't be into a girl joining the Saturday rec center game.

"Um, I don't know about any, uh, games," you stutter.

"You know," she says, sounding a little angry, "I never pegged you for a liar, Phil Halverson." She turns to look you in the eyes. "I know you play at the rec center. If you didn't want to play ball with me, you could just say so." She starts to walk away from you.

"No, wait," you call out and run after her. "I do, I just don't know about the guys." She stops walking but doesn't turn around. You tell her that you have a hoop at your house. "You could come over and we could play one-on-one in my driveway," you offer.

Did that sound desperate? You hope not.

"Well," she says, slowly turning back around. "It would be nice to have someone to play with again. Like I said before, I haven't had anyone to shoot hoops with since my brother left for the Navy two years ago."

You tell Ellie to come over Sunday afternoon, because the weather is supposed to be nice. You can't believe this is really happening. You've had a crush on Ellie Burkoski since third grade! For the first time in months, you're actually glad your dad will be working overtime on the weekend, and you know your mom won't bother you, because she'll probably be in her room all day. At least, that's what you figure.

Go on to the next page.

On Sunday morning, you're surprised to find your mom in the kitchen. She's actually cooking something too.

"Hey, mom, whatcha doin'?"

"Good morning," she smiles. *Mom's cooking and smiling. What's going on here?*

"I was really proud of you the other night," she continues. "That was a great play."

"Well, at least it went in, right?" You laugh off her compliment.

"That was a tough decision you made. It was the right thing for your team, and you didn't worry about what people would say. Honestly, honey, I think I can learn a thing or two from you."

You're not exactly sure what she means, but if she's smiling again, then you're happy.

When Ellie shows up, you grab your ball from the garage. You're thinking you'll go easy on her, but she blows you away immediately. The sweet, sometimes shy girl you like becomes an aggressive and very worthy opponent on the court. You're impressed.

"Hey, where'd you learn to play again?"

"My older brother," she replies. "You know," she pauses a moment, "he taught me how to make an overhand free throw too."

Your face starts to feel a little hot. Maybe you do care what people think.

"Your underhand toss was smart," she continues. "But, if you

Go on to the next page.

want, I could show you what my brother taught me."

A girl helping you shoot? Not likely. But then, you stop to really consider it. Nope, your mom *was* right; you don't care what people think, especially if Ellie can help you knock down that darn free throw.

THE END

You wish Jesse would either get aggressive or give up on lay-ups, and you'd like to say so, but you don't want him thinking that you're always telling him what to do. Uh-oh, here he goes again.

You slide in there, ready for the rebound. Dan Connors is between you and the hoop, trying to box you out, but you fake right and slip around him on the other side. Now you're ready on the weak side. Jesse shoots and it rolls across the back rim, right toward you. You get the ball, power it back up to the hoop for a bank shot. The Fixer strikes again.

"Nice save," Tommy calls out.

Just then, a loud crash comes from the ceiling. You think it was something in the abandoned offices above the gym. You guys snuck in there once to investigate. There were old filing cabinets, typewriters, some cool old photos of rec center sports teams from back when your grandparents were kids, and tons and tons of broken gym equipment. You guys had a lot of fun playing with it that day, until Matty cut his arm on one of the old weight machines. You haven't been up there since, but you figure that crash was some old exercise machine falling down.

Then, the fire alarm goes off. For a minute, you all stop and stare at each other. Why would they do a fire drill with only a few people here?

They wouldn't. This is not a drill.

Mrs. Hughes, the rec center nurse, runs into the gym.

"Boys, come this way," she shouts. "We need to evacuate the

Go on to the next page.

building, now!"

It's incredible. The whole top of the rec center is on fire, and there are two boys on the edge of the roof yelling for help. You recognize them as Jesse's friends, Justin and Cal. A couple of firefighters climb up long ladders to rescue them. Others direct hoses at the top-floor windows, sending giant streams of water into the building, and you guys get to watch the whole thing. The police even interview you.

On the way home, you try to think of a good way to talk with Jesse about his friends.

"Those guys are kinda messed up," you say. "I don't want to tell you what to do, but . . . "

"Don't even, Phil, they're my friends," he defends.

"C'mon, dude, they tried to burn down the rec center." You both can't help but laugh a little; it's crazy for him to stick up for them right now.

"I guess they *are* kinda messed up," he admits.

"You know, if we hung out more," you offer, "I could help you get more comfortable with contact." He's just nervous because he got swatted once.

"I guess," he says and shrugs, but you can tell that something has shifted.

Who knows what'll happen with Jesse, or even with your parents for that matter, but at least for today you got to be the fixer.

THE END

You can't let Jesse get busted for having cigarettes. Your parents have really been hard on him lately, especially your dad, and this might be the final straw. He drives you crazy, but you don't want to see him shipped off to some military school or something.

"Cigarettes?!" Mrs. Doyle is astonished.

"They're mine," you blurt out.

"Give them to me," Mrs. Doyle demands, and Jesse hands them over. "Were you trying to get him to smoke with you?" she asks you, sounding exasperated.

"No, I . . . " but you're not sure what to say.

She tells you it doesn't matter. This is a huge policy violation, and she's taking you to the principal's office.

You've never gone to the principal's office before. You're the good kid. The kid who gets good grades, the kid who teachers like, the basketball star. Maybe you didn't think this through very well; you may have just thrown away all your dreams. Coach will kick you off the team for sure now, and what are your mom and dad going to do?

Mr. Diggle is not in his office when you get there, so you have to just sit and wait for him in what everyone calls "the box of shame" – the area right outside his office. If you could think of a way to protect Jesse and save yourself you would, but you're stuck. You can feel all the blood leaving your face. Your head feels light, and your stomach is in your throat. For a moment, the world spins, then everything goes black. You pass out.

Go on to the next page.

Next thing you know, you wake up on the floor, the right side of your face stinging with pain. Coach is leaning over you.

"You alright, Halverson?" he asks, helping you into a chair.

You're not really sure about your body, but you know everything else is wrecked.

"I messed up, Coach."

"I know, kid, I heard." He sounds so disappointed, and this stings worse than the pain in your face.

Mrs. Doyle comes back in with Mr. Diggle and an ice pack, and you all go into the principal's office. Coach stands with his back to you, staring out the window. Mrs. Doyle motions for you to sit down and takes the chair next to you. Mr. Diggle sizes you up while he cleans the lenses of his glasses, then presses them up the bridge of his nose with one chubby finger.

"Mr. Halverson," he says in his unnaturally squeaky voice, "it's come to my attention that in addition to this incident with the cigarettes, you've been late for school, and your grades are slipping in some classes. What do you have to say for yourself, sir?"

Aside from the bit about the cigarettes, the rest is all true. And what *can* you say? *Sorry, my family's a mess and so am I?* You decide you won't say anything; you'll just take whatever comes.

Just then, Jesse runs into the office. He's got a strange look on his face.

"They were mine," he says. "The cigarettes were mine."

GO TO PAGE 39.

You don't want to talk about your messed up family with Coach. He wouldn't understand. No one would. And now he's looking at you in that way that seems like he's reading your mind. It freaks you out a little bit.

"It's nothing, Coach," you lie. "I just stayed up too late last night and overslept this morning." You promise it won't happen again.

"You know how I feel about academics, Phil. A good athlete trains his body *and* his mind. He eats well, drinks lots of water, and . . . "

" . . . he sleeps eight hours a night," you finish his sentence for him. "I know, Coach. I'm really sorry."

He tells you that, even if you are one of his best players, he won't think twice about benching you if you don't get your act together. You promise him again that you will, and hustle into the locker room. You're done thinking about what's going on at home; you just want to play basketball.

The next day, you make it to school on time and the game gives you plenty to focus on. It's the first time the two schools have faced each other since the all-county tournament last season, when the Lions won. The gymnasium will be packed; it always is when the Dragons and Lions compete. You'll give them a good show, because it's a pretty fair matchup, and you and your guys are pumped, but it's going to be a tough one.

There will be some interesting battles on the floor tonight. You have 12 guys on your team but, even though Coach is usually really

Go on to the next page.

good about giving everyone court time, when you play the Lions, the best players don't really warm the bench too much. You start going over some of the matchups in your head.

The Lions' point guard, Skip Davis, doesn't turn the ball over often, but you've got Matty, who's really improved his speed and decision making. Dan Connors is the Lions' best all-around player, but he'll be matched by Ashton, who is by far your most explosive player. Tommy is a mad scorer and can change a game quickly when he gets going, even if Jimmy "The Wall" McCue may get some tough rebounds. Then there's the offense. They may have a great one, but you've got an aggressive defense. Jason Blackwell is their most dangerous shooter, but you're a choice defender and you pestered Blackwell all season long last year.

Their defense wasn't tremendous last season, but a lot can change in a year, and you wonder what you'll be facing out there. You don't have to wonder for long though, because it's time to hit the court.

The Dragons are ready to do battle. Unfortunately, the Lions are the ones on fire tonight. They're really guarding that hoop. Their defense swarms you and keeps you back. You just can't get around them, even though you keep trying.

The Dragons are a determined bunch though, and by the time the closing seconds creep up, your team is only trailing by two points. Skip Davis, the Lions' power forward, misses a couple of free throws. Just 10 seconds left on the clock. Now you have a chance.

Go on to the next page.

Tommy passes to Ashton, working the ball around to the wing. He fakes left and passes to Matt, who moves toward the net but gets blocked by Jimmy McCue, so he passes to you. You take a jump shot, but Dan Connors jumps too and, just as you release the ball, his elbow tags your shoulder – hard. The ball drops through the net. The buzzer sounds. You're tied.

That foul hurts in more ways than one. Now you're in pain and worried about trying to make a shot you can never pull off. You know that you can't make the free throw overhand, the only way you can hit your free throws consistently is to take them "granny style" by shooting underhand, but you've never had the guts to try it in a game because, if you miss, you might never hear the end of it.

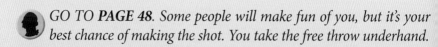 *GO TO **PAGE 48**. Some people will make fun of you, but it's your best chance of making the shot. You take the free throw underhand.*

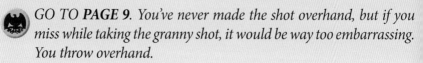 *GO TO **PAGE 9**. You've never made the shot overhand, but if you miss while taking the granny shot, it would be way too embarrassing. You throw overhand.*

You think you could probably get the ball back, because these guys seem like oafs, but one of them already pushed Jesse and you don't want him to get hurt.

"Whatever, man," you say, and grab your brother. You figure you'll head to your grandparents' house and chill out in your tree fort for a bit. They only live around the corner, and maybe the Lindonville guys will get bored once you leave and forget about your ball.

Pepi barks as you walk past him. He's a strange little poodle who sits on top of his doghouse, like Snoopy. As you climb the ladder to the tree fort, you can see your Grandma Kay and Papa inside the house.

The tree fort used to be your favorite place to hang out. You and Jesse practically lived there. Every Sunday, when you went to your grandparents' house for supper, you and he would spend hours up there, reading, playing video games, or sometimes just lying on the old rug your Grandma put in, watching the way the sunlight peeked around the leaves.

Both your grandparents helped build the tree fort, and you'll never forget how Papa smashed his thumb nailing the very last ladder rung. He hopped around the yard yelping, which made Pepi start hopping and yelping too. None of you meant to, but you all fell over laughing at the spectacle. You miss hanging out with your grandparents.

Just then, you hear a soft voice from below.

"Are you two comfortable?" your grandma asks.

You motion to Jesse to be quiet and consider not answering her

Go on to the next page.

for a minute, but you realize you're busted and give in.

"Hi Grandma," you both call down.

Before you know it, she's up the ladder and in the tree fort with you. She wants to know what you're doing out so late and why you're up in the tree fort. You decide to skip the bit about the guys who almost pummeled your brother, and you just tell her that everything is weird and changing at home. She asks if you want to hear a story.

Grandma tells great stories, and she always has titles for them too, which make them seem like epic adventures, even if they're just about losing an earring or finding a dog. Like the day Papa smashed his thumb – she calls that "The Great Treehouse Finale."

"This is the story of 'The Biggest Change,' boys, and I'm not sure if I've told it to you before. Did either of you know that your old grandma played hoops back in college?"

"No," you and Jesse say in unison, both of you clearly surprised.

"Well, I did," she continues, "and I was good too."

She adjusts the collar of her jacket and pulls her feet up under her so she's sitting cross-legged. You can tell this is going to be a good one.

"Now, before I tell you the end, I have to tell you the beginning," she says. "I started playing basketball back in the early 1960s. I was just a year or two younger than you, Jesse. You know, back then, the rules were different for girls and boys. First off, we had to wear heavy skirts, which were not easy to run in – not that they wanted us running," she says, rolling her eyes. "We played six-on-six, with two rovers. The two

Go on to the next page.

stationary guards weren't even allowed to move past half court, and the two stationary forwards could only shoot and rebound. We were only allowed to dribble three times in a row." She says while holding up three fingers for emphasis. "Only *three*. My college coach used to say that at least that set-up was good for fast breaks."

She giggles and stares out the window for a moment, as if remembering a part of the story that she doesn't intend to share.

"Anyway, by the time I got to college in the early 70s, things had started to change. We were playing five-on-five, and we could all move around the full court." She pauses, and sits up straight. "I even got one of the first college scholarships for women athletes," she says proudly.

You and Jesse had no idea your grandma was this cool.

She goes on to say that "The Biggest Change" came in February 1975. Her team from Immaculata College played against Queens College in front of about 12 thousand fans. It was the first-ever women's college game played at Madison Square Garden.

"It was amazing," she says.

She tells you some of the exciting highlights, gesturing wildly as she describes different plays. Then she takes a deep breath and is quiet for a moment.

"It was toward the end of the second half." She looks down. "I went for a jump shot and got fouled. When I landed, my ankle snapped, and then the gal who fouled me fell on it. I knew I was out, but I didn't realize I was out for good."

Go on to the next page.

"Why?" Jesse asks.

She tells you that the injury caused permanent damage. It affects her ability to run even now. Then she tells you about the handsome young medic who tended to her injury. She tells you that he took especially good care of her and made her laugh more than anyone ever had. She tells you that they fell in love.

"Wait a minute," you say. "Who won the game?"

"We did," she says, smiling, "59 to 52."

She tells you the injury broke her heart as well as her ankle, because basketball was her life, but she'd do it all again, just to meet your papa.

"Sometimes," she says, "change seems like the worst thing, but you never know what good things may come."

You're not sure if you could say that about what's been going on with you, but you figure you'll have to wait and see. Right now, you just hope grandma won't want to tell your story.

THE END

You go to Ashton's for strategizing rather than go with your mom. Coach has a "no looking back" policy. He says it's good to learn from your mistakes, but you can only do that if you're looking forward. Still, you wish the stuff with your family wasn't so distracting.

When you get to Ashton's house, you feel better. Despite losing, everyone is in a good mood, and there's pepperoni pizza – your favorite. Plus, some girls from school are visiting Ashton's sister, Jeannine. You see Ellie Burkoski sitting on the couch, and she even waves.

You've known Ellie since you were in diapers, and you've liked her almost as long. After you and the guys do some strategizing about the next time you face the Lions, you watch TV with the girls. Somehow, you get into a conversation with Ellie about tonight's game, and you're surprised by how much she knows.

"Wow, you know a lot about basketball," you say.

"My dad played college ball, so it's kind of a thing at my house," she explains, and says, "Hey, you should come over and watch a game with us sometime. My dad will crack you up."

You can't believe that Ellie Burkoski just invited you over to watch basketball. You're wondering if you should pinch yourself, but there's no need – Ellie slugs you in the arm and says, "Listen, I gotta go, but I'll see you in school."

You're beginning to really appreciate Coach's policy on looking

Go on to the next page.

forward. You may not have won the game tonight, but you're definitely feeling like a winner.

THE END

You let go of your shoulder and roll it back a few times, then forward. It really does hurt, but not as badly as you were making it seem.

"Actually, Coach," you say, "I think I can do it."

"Good, kid, I'm glad to hear it," he replies. "And listen, there's no pressure here, just go out there and do your best."

You nod and thank him, but you're still super nervous. Maybe it's the packed auditorium. One side filled with people wearing green and white from Chesterton, and the other filled with people in gold and blue from Lindonville. Some people are waiving pom-poms. There are signs that say, "GO DRAGONS" or "GO LIONS." Some people even have their faces painted. *Sure, there's no pressure.* Regardless, you're committed now.

You step out onto the court. You try to relax with some deep breaths and, in your head, you keep repeating, *I can do it, I can do it, I can do it*. You stare at the basket and spin the ball between both hands and slightly up into the air. You bend your knees, dribble the ball exactly three times, grab it, take another deep breath, and shoot. The ball hits the rim and rolls around it, not once, not twice, but three times. No one is breathing. The whole auditorium is silent. Then, the impossible happens: It goes in. The Dragons win the game!

You can't believe that just happened. You actually made a free throw. Imagine if you hadn't been willing to take a chance.

THE END

Walking with Ellie Burkoski to get ice cream at Two Scoops is very tempting, but you apologize to her and run over to catch up with your buddies. Part of you can't believe you just turned down a chance to hang out with the cutest girl you know. You've only had a crush on her forever. But you want to celebrate with your team.

Out in the parking lot, a few Lions fans are standing around grumbling about the loss. They're older and bigger than you guys.

"Hey, Granny, need some help to your car?" one of them yells.

"Better be careful," another one says, "or you might fall and not be able to get up."

They start laughing and pretending to walk like old people, hunched over with canes.

"I thought he was going to take a dump out there," one of them says, making grunting noises and exaggerating the squatting position you took to make the toss.

"Forget this," Tommy says, throwing down his gym bag and starting toward them.

"Just leave it, Tom," you say. "I'm in enough trouble with Coach for being late to school. I can't afford to get into a fight too. Besides, they're just being sore losers."

"Yeah," Tommy agrees, and then yells toward them, "They're just *losers.*"

It was a good call to ignore them too, because Coach saw what was happening. He walks over to you guys and tells you all how proud

Go on to the next page.

he is of you.

After ice cream, you head home. Your mom and dad are in the kitchen, and they're *talking* instead of yelling.

"Great job tonight, honey," your mom says, though she looks really sad.

"That was an interesting play," your dad says. "Nice work."

"Thanks," you smile, wondering what's going on. "Where's Jesse?" you ask.

"In his room, and that's where he's staying. Your brother's in pretty deep, bud."

You know better than to press for more. Whatever he's done, it must be serious. Ever since your parents started fighting, you've been distracted, but Jesse's been getting into trouble.

The next morning, Jesse leaves before you, but he's not on the bus. You see him a block from school with some shady kids. You don't want to be late again, but you wait for him anyway. You just want to make sure he's not doing something monumentally stupid.

"What's up, Jess?"

"Nothing. What do you care?"

Mrs. Doyle yells for you to get to class and starts walking toward you.

Jesse's hiding something in his pocket. It's a pack of cigarettes. You both grab for them at the same time, and they fall to the ground just in time to land at Mrs. Doyle's feet. What are you going to do?

 GO TO **PAGE 24**. *You take the blame for your brother, because you know he's one bad deed away from disciplinary school.*

 GO TO **PAGE 18**. *You can't take the fall for him. You're already on thin ice with Coach, and you're worried that Jesse needs more help than you can give anyway.*

You want Jesse to know that you are paying attention to him. Even though it's dark, and your parents definitely would not go for it, you think it would be good for both of you to get out of the house and play some hoops. There's a park near your grandparents' house, where the court is lit-up at night, and it's only about a 10-minute walk. Plus, it's not particularly cold for November.

"I can't believe you want to do something that could get us in trouble," Jesse laughs when you tell him your plan.

"I know, but I really need to get out of here for a bit," you say.

Jesse practically runs out the door. Looks like he's ready to get away, too.

It's been a while since you two played ball, but you fall into a pretty easy rhythm. He's no match for your defense, but he can dribble and he's fast. You're having so much fun that you don't notice a couple guys walk up, until one runs between you and snags the ball from Jesse.

"Hey," Jesse yells, but the guy just laughs.

They're older, and you can tell they're from Lindonville because of their jackets. They look like football players, maybe sophomores or juniors. The guy who grabbed the ball pushes Jesse out of the way and motions for his friend to come over.

"Give it back," you demand.

"Think you can take it?" he taunts.

Jesse looks scared. You could run around the corner to your grandparents' house, but you think you can get the ball from him.

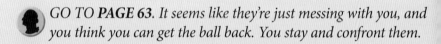

GO TO **PAGE 63**. *It seems like they're just messing with you, and you think you can get the ball back. You stay and confront them.*

GO TO **PAGE 29**. *You're not taking chances. You grab Jesse and head to your grandparents'.*

Everyone looks at Jesse. There's something desperate about him, and you feel helpless. Then Coach starts to speak.

"I'd like a moment with Principal Diggle," he says. "You boys wait outside."

Mrs. Doyle says she'll wait with you and Jesse. She says your parents are on their way, but she doesn't sound as menacing as before. She sounds almost apologetic.

When your parents arrive, Coach quickly ushers them into Mr. Diggle's office. They don't even have a chance to speak to you and Jesse. You see the looks on their faces though. Mom's been crying and Dad looks super ticked off. You and Jesse don't say anything or even make eye contact for what feels like forever. Eventually, Jesse breaks the silence.

"What's gonna happen?" he asks.

"I don't know," you say honestly, "but I don't think it's going to be good."

The longer you sit there, the worse you imagine the consequences. A few times, you work up the nerve to turn your head to the side, just far enough so that you can peek a glimpse into the principal's office and see what's going on. At one point, you see your dad standing and it looks like he might start yelling. Your dad is a big man; he can be intimidating, and you hope he doesn't lose his cool. Your poor mom is crying again. A few minutes later, you sneak another glance, everyone is seated and calm now. It looks like Coach is talking.

Go on to the next page.

When your parents finally walk out, it's weird. They look relieved. Your mom says she'll see you at home. Your dad gives you each a nod. You may have even caught a slight smile. Then Coach motions to you.

Principal Diggle stands behind his desk wringing his hands. He looks uncomfortable, like he ate something bitter. He clearly doesn't like giving the floor over, but Coach is the kind of guy you give the floor. He's the kind of person who commands respect – probably because he gives it.

"Listen boys," Coach says, "we know things have been kind of rough at home."

What? That's what they were talking about? Now you're the one feeling uncomfortable.

"When families have problems," he continues, "it often affects everything in your life, but we want you to know you don't have to deal with it alone."

When he says "we" he motions to the principal, but you can tell Diggle doesn't consider himself part of that "we." You're so grateful that Coach is the one talking.

"I'll let your folks fill you in on the particulars," Coach says, "but you're all going to see a counselor to help work things out. And here's what's going to happen at school . . . "

"*You're* getting detention," Principal Diggle blurts out at Jesse.

"Yes," Coach says calmly, "and you'll spend it with me."

You're glad Jesse will be with Coach. You're not so sure about the

Go on to the next page.

counselor thing though. Still, your parents did look relieved. You'll just have to see what happens next.

THE END

You hate to disappoint Coach, and you hate to lie even more, but you just know you can't make the free throw. Plus, you're determined not to cause your team to lose. You vow to yourself that you're going to practice hard and, next time, the free throw will be yours. Coach asks one of the other guys to grab an ice pack for you, and then he sends in Matty to take the shot. You're glad too. Matt hits his free throws about eighty percent of the time.

You sit on the bench hunched over and pressing the ice to your shoulder. The minor pain caused by Dan's elbow gives way to the distinct sting of having something frozen against your skin. It slowly begins to numb. The icepack bleeds drops of water that trickle down your back. You can't help feeling some regret over your decision to play up the injury. You can't help wondering what would have happened if you'd tried. Realizing that the person you've disappointed is actually yourself, you feel even worse. You're going to master that free throw if it's the last thing you do.

Meanwhile, Matty is out on the court. The auditorium is silent. Without hesitation, and with total confidence, he makes a perfect shot. The Dragons win the game. The guys all slap him on the back and congratulate him. Behind you, the bleachers erupt with cheers, and someone starts the Dragons' rally cry. You join in, but it's half-hearted at best. You're happy that your team won; you just can't seem to get in the celebratory spirit.

You hear your mom call your name and, when you look, she's

Go on to the next page.

frowning and pointing to her shoulder. You nod in response. It's just her and Jesse, but you can't help thinking about your dad. He used to be the person who would help you with a difficult play or move. You wish he wasn't so checked out lately. Between family and basketball, things are feeling really far out of whack.

"I'm taking everyone to Two Scoops," Coach says.

"Not me, Coach," you say, shaking your head, but trying not to make a big deal of it.

"Does it hurt that bad, Fixer?" Tommy wants to know.

"Yeah, I dunno, I just . . . " You don't really know what to say.

That's when Coach walks over and looks like he's X-raying you with his eyes again. You already feel bad enough; you just want to get out of there.

"Halverson," he says. "I know things can seem pretty black and white sometimes. Either you make the shot or you don't make the shot. Either you win or you lose. But it's not really that simple," he says. Then he continues, "Sometimes, you get more out of just trying, regardless of the result, so you have to be willing to go for it and fail." He puts his arm around you and says, "And don't worry, kid, there will be plenty of opportunities to do just that."

THE END

You're bummed about losing the game and the dumb free throw, and you'd like to just go over Ashton's to avoid your family, but your mom looks like a train wreck. You can tell she's upset about something Jesse has done and you want to see if you can help.

Normally, you and your brother would yell "shotgun" for the front seat, but tonight he slips in the back without a word. Whatever he did, it must be bad. Your mom's hands shake when she puts them on the wheel. She's really upset. That's it. You can't handle the suspense anymore.

"Okay, what the heck is going on?"

"Not now, Phil," your mom says, slipping the key into the ignition.

"Mom, your hands are shaking and you were holding onto him in there like he might escape if you let go. What happened?"

Your mom turns the car off and shuts her eyes. She takes a deep breath. Jesse makes himself as small as possible in the corner of the backseat and doesn't say anything.

"Your brother was caught shoplifting liquor from a convenient store," she says.

"How? They keep that stuff behind the register."

"Well, it seems he had some help from his friends, before they ran away and left him," she says sarcastically.

Your mom tells you that the store manager called her. Turns out, they went to high school together, so he decided to let Jesse off with a warning.

Go on to the next page.

When you get home, Jesse goes straight to his room. Your mom heads to the kitchen and pours herself a glass of water, but she can barely steady the glass.

"I don't know what we're going to do about him," she says, putting her head in her hands.

"What I can do to help?" you ask, sitting down next to her.

"Oh, sweetie," she says. "Don't worry. Your dad will be home soon and we'll handle it. You just go finish up your homework, okay?"

A little while later, you can hear your dad railing on Jesse, threatening to send him to a disciplinary school. You try to focus on your homework, but it's difficult. Jesse definitely messed up but, maybe if your dad were around more, your brother wouldn't get in trouble all the time. You wonder if maybe you should talk to Jesse.

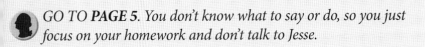

GO TO **PAGE 5**. *You don't know what to say or do, so you just focus on your homework and don't talk to Jesse.*

GO TO **PAGE 54**. *You talk to Jesse, because you think maybe you can help somehow, and you hate seeing your little brother get into so much trouble.*

You grab the ball and call a timeout.

"Come here, guys," you say.

You don't want to single out Jesse and make him regret coming. It was difficult enough to get him here. You decide to make it a tactical speech and keep it general.

"Alright," you say, "we know what Dan's up to, but this guy, Ed, he's a wild card. He's short and fast, so stay away from isolation plays when he's guarding you. Try to use pick and rolls to force a switch, okay?"

They all nod.

"What if I want to go for a lay-up?" Jesse asks.

"Dude, you cannot make a lay-up. You're too timid," Matty says.

"I'm not timid," Jesse argues and starts to get in Matty's face.

"Whoah, little turd, don't even start with me," Matty says leaning in. Jesse has always annoyed him. "You're lucky we even agreed to let you play with us today."

"Whatever, I don't even want to be here," Jesse says, but doesn't back down.

This stinks. You don't want to get between your brother and best friend, but if push comes to shove, you're going to pick Jesse.

"Listen, Jess," you interject, casually stepping between them. "I just want you to think about what's best for our team."

"Why are you always telling me what to do, Phil? I'm sick of it!"

"I get it," you say and lead him away from the guys for a minute. In a lower voice you say, "Look, I'm not trying to tell you what to do.

Go on to the next page.

Really," you promise. "I'm trying to give you advice on how to use your strengths."

You tell him you understand. You get that he likes to drive the lane and go for a lay-up, but he's more confident with his outside shots. You see his face begin to soften as he realizes your not just saying he stinks. You encourage him some more and put your arm around his shoulder.

Just as you turn to walk back, you see Cal and Justin standing in the doorway to the gym.

"I got this," Tommy says as he and Matt jog by you.

Jesse wants to go over, but you convince him not to. You're not sure what Tommy says to them, but luckily, they take off.

A moment later, you're back on the court. Matty has the ball. Neither you nor Ash are open for a pass. Matty hesitates for a moment, almost losing the ball, but then he reluctantly passes to Jesse, who takes a three from the corner that wins the game.

"Great job out there today," you say to Jesse on the way home.

"Thanks," he says, clearly proud of himself. "And thanks for the good advice too."

Wow. Did Jesse actually just thank you? Unbelievable – he won the game *and* thanked you for your advice. If that happened, maybe you'll see pigs fly too. At this point, anything's possible.

THE END

It was a seriously tough decision, but you have much better odds at making the shot underhand. So, the granny toss it is. Ugh. What are you doing?

You stretch your shoulder a bit to work out the knot from that elbow you took. Then, you step up to the free-throw line. You take your stance. Feet shoulder width apart, knees bent. You hold the ball in both hands. There are whispers as people figure out what you're doing, and someone even snickers. You block it all out, clearing your mind. You've got this. Next, you lift up and release. A million years pass before the ball reaches the hoop. You can feel your body shaking with anticipation. Then, swoosh. It goes in and the crowd goes wild!

"Hey, Granny," someone calls out from the Lions' side of the bleachers, "nice shot." Your face heats up with embarrassment.

"Don't listen to 'em, kid," Coach says. "You did it just like Rick Barry."

"Who?" you say.

"Rick Barry," he repeats. "He's one of the best players in NBA history."

"I've never heard of him," you admit.

"Well," Coach says, "he's the only player to lead the NCAA, ABA, and NBA in scoring for an individual season. His ABA points-per-game average is *still* the highest career total for a player in any professional league, and *he* played back in the 70s, kid. *And*," he pauses, "one of the other things he's best known for is shooting highly

Go on to the next page.

accurate underhanded free throws."

Whoa. That's pretty cool.

"Ice cream at Two Scoops is on me," Coach says.

You look around for your mom. When you see her, you motion that you're going with the team and she gives you the "okay" sign. That's when you realize Ellie Burkoski is standing right in front of you, smiling.

"Hey, Phil," she says. "Congratulations."

Ellie has the prettiest bright green eyes and cute freckles over the top of her nose. You've liked her forever, and she wants to know if you'll walk with her to Two Scoops.

 GO TO **PAGE 52**. A win against the Lions, a walk with Ellie, and ice cream – what more could you ask for? You take a walk with the girl of your dreams.

 GO TO **PAGE 36**. A walk with Ellie is tempting, but the guys are calling for you, and you should celebrate with your team.

Coach wants to know what's wrong, but it's all so weird and confusing, and you're not exactly sure what to say. You stare at the floor, wishing you hadn't been late for school, wishing Jesse had been ready on time, wishing your mom had gotten you up and made breakfast, wishing you hadn't been up so late with your head pounding, wishing your parents weren't fighting constantly. You just wish things were different.

"Phil, you can talk to me about anything," he says.

"Yeah, I know, but . . . "

"Is everything okay at home?" he asks. *How did he know?*

"Um," you hesitate, then tell him, "not really, no."

"Listen," he says. "If you talk to me about it, maybe I can help."

Coach is very patient while you try to find the words. It's impressive, seeing as how you have a big game to get ready for, but also his calm and patience help you feel a little less embarrassed.

You tell him that your parents have been fighting non-stop for the past four months. You don't even know what they're fighting about half the time. Jesse has been a mess. You can't believe how much trouble a 10-year-old can cause and get into. You've been trying to take care of your mom, who's been really sad. You've been trying to reel in Jesse, before he gets completely out of hand. You don't even know what to say about your dad. He's just never around anymore.

The whole time you talk, Coach is silent. He just nods his head here and there, so you know he's getting it. You had no idea what a

Go on to the next page.

relief it would be just to say it all out loud.

"You know, kid," Coach says when you finish, "I never call you 'Fixer' because it's not one person's job to fix things for everyone. Seems like that's what you're trying to do."

"I just . . . " you start.

"Now, hold on a sec," Coach says. "It's my turn."

He's just going to tell you school is important and blah, blah, blah. Maybe Coach doesn't understand after all.

"My mom was an alcoholic," he says.

What does that mean? An alcoholic is just someone who drinks too much, right?

Coach tells you she was a functioning alcoholic. She had a job, kept a home, and raised three kids. But, because of her drinking, he always felt like he had to take care of her. He tells you that he felt hopeless and frustrated for a long time, like he could never do enough. Until, that is, he got some help.

"I know your situation is different," he says, "but it sounds like you could use some help too. I'd like you to see one of the school counselors. I'll even go with you," he offers.

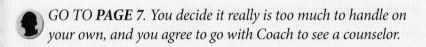 GO TO **PAGE 7**. *You decide it really is too much to handle on your own, and you agree to go with Coach to see a counselor.*

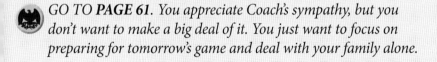 GO TO **PAGE 61**. *You appreciate Coach's sympathy, but you don't want to make a big deal of it. You just want to focus on preparing for tomorrow's game and deal with your family alone.*

You can't believe it. You're actually walking with Ellie Burkoski. You're walking, you realize, but you're not talking. What do you talk to girls about anyway? You walk in silence for about five minutes, and you're glad it only takes 10 to get to Two Scoops. Still, you feel like you should say something.

"So, what was your favorite part of the game tonight?" you ask.

"Your free throw, of course," she says.

You didn't mean to fish for a compliment. She probably thinks your full of yourself now. Great, just great.

"Rick Barry used to shoot like that," she smiles. "My dad says there's no shame in getting the job done right."

She knows about Rick Barry?

"Yeah," you chuckle. "Well, it wasn't my first choice, but it worked, right?"

"Definitely," she says.

"How do you know about Rick Barry?" you ask.

"I can name all of the greatest players in NBA history," she says matter-of-factly.

"Seriously?"

"Yeah, my dad taught me," she says.

Wow. Very cool.

"Shaq's always been my guy, but now I'm rethinking it," you say. "He couldn't make a free throw either." You both laugh.

"I know a lot of basketball trivia," she says, "but what I really like

Go on to the next page.

is playing."

Your middle school doesn't have a girls' team, but the other middle school near the Hanaford River does. It's called Chesterton-on-Hanaford. The high school has a girls' team too, so it's strange that you guys don't have one.

"Why don't we have a girls' team?" you ask.

"There used to be one," she says, "but there hasn't been enough interest. I asked my folks if I could transfer to C-o-H this year, because I really want to be ready for high school, but there's some weird districting thing. We'd have to move for me to go there."

She sounds pretty defeated, and you wish you had a way to cheer her up.

"That really stinks," you say.

"Yeah," she agrees. Then she gets a funny look on her face, like she's had a brilliant idea. "I hear sometimes there are pick-up games on the weekends. You know, down at the rec center. Have you heard anything about that?" she asks.

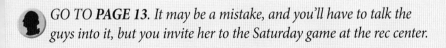
GO TO **PAGE 13**. It may be a mistake, and you'll have to talk the guys into it, but you invite her to the Saturday game at the rec center.

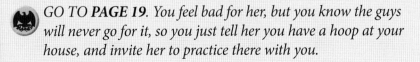
GO TO **PAGE 19**. You feel bad for her, but you know the guys will never go for it, so you just tell her you have a hoop at your house, and invite her to practice there with you.

Your dad finally stops yelling. He knocks on your door, but you say you're busy with homework and he heads downstairs. You walk over to Jesse's room. The door is open and he is sitting on the floor in the corner crying. His face is bright red and wet from tears. It really makes you angry to see him like this, but you're still also a little ticked off that he would pull such a stupid stunt. *What was he thinking?*

"Just leave me alone, Phil," he says through sobs.

"I'm not here to give you a hard time, I just want to talk."

Sitting on the floor across from him, you lean back against the wall. Jesse's room is like a cave. He has the windows covered with blankets and all he ever does is play video games. You like video games too, but that's *all* he does. You think it's hopeful that he still has the LeBron poster you gave him for his birthday on the wall.

"You still like LeBron?" you ask, trying to break the ice a little.

"I guess," he says.

"You guess? Dude, he's won championships, gold medals, and he led the Heat on a 27-game winning streak. He's the best."

"Why are you asking me about basketball?" he wants to know.

"I dunno," you say, "we used to talk about basketball when we hung out more. Now, you're always with Cal and Justin."

"They're my friends," he defends.

"Yeah, friends who nearly got you arrested," you say.

"Just get out," he half growls and half pleads.

"I didn't come to fight, Jess. We need a fifth for our pick-up game

Go on to the next page.

this weekend."

"I don't want to hang out with your jerky friends, and I don't need you to babysit me," he says defiantly.

You really do need a fifth, so you remind him that he's known the twins practically since birth. They'll be happy to see him. Well, Matt might not. He and Jesse always get into it, but Tommy will.

"Remember two summers ago?" you say. "We shot hoops in the driveway every day. On the weekend, we played at the court near Grandma and Papa's."

He nods, "Yeah, so what?"

"Well, we had fun. That's all."

He thinks about it for a while, but finally agrees. He'll come.

On Saturday, you meet the guys at the rec center. They're cool with Jesse playing. You're up against Dan Connors, from the Lions, three of his buddies, and his cousin Ed, who's visiting from Florida. Luckily, Jesse's got speed, and he's playing a pretty good game. Unfortunately, he keeps going for a lay-up, but he's so afraid of contact, he can't do it.

 GO TO **PAGE 46**. *You call a timeout, hoping you can coach Jesse without making him feel like you're telling him what to do.*

 GO TO **PAGE 22**. *You let the game play out and hope Jesse will realize that his lay-ups are about as good as your free throws.*

Jesse is feeling courageous, and who are you to stand in his way? Besides, you have a plan. The only problem is that Jesse doesn't know the plan and you're not sure how to let him in on it without letting the Lindonville thugs in on it too.

First, you try to signal him with your eyes and facial expressions, but he looks at you like you're crazy.

Next, you cough to draw his attention, and then try to use subtle hand gestures to convey your master plan. But that falls flat too.

Meanwhile, the guys from Lindonville are still playing the game like it's a form of keep-away. You don't care though, as soon as Jesse knows what you're thinking, you can execute and escape.

At one point the guy who first took the ball actually dribbles it for a minute. Then, he seems to get a little cocky and tries for a behind-the-back pass. It goes nowhere near his buddy, and Jesse grabs it. For a minute, you think this is your big break, but the guy who was intended to receive the pass charges and tumbles into Jesse, knocking him down. Then, the big dufus lands on top of him, and Jesse yells out in pain. It's his arm.

"Jesse, are you okay?" you rush over to him.

Luckily, it seems like just a sprain. And although that qualifies your team to get the ball, these guys are still not playing by any actual rules. If they would just let go of the ball, you could get it.

Finally, the best idea comes to you. When you and Jesse were younger, you went to summer camp, where you learned a very simple,

Go on to the next page.

but secret, language. You wonder if Jesse remembers it. You sure hope so.

"Feedomkin!" you yell to see if he responds.

"Yeah," Jesse calls back, raising his fists in the air. It seems he at least remembers "freedom," and you are hoping he remembers the rest.

The other guys look at you like you're a weirdo, but continue bobbing and weaving with the ball, passing it to one another at close range, without dribbling at all – basically handing it off to each other.

"Iggle tippin and charrufin," you say to Jesse. (*I will take and run.*)

It takes him a moment, but then his face brightens with recognition.

"Ubu charrufin dastuni," you continue. "Charrufin humbo." (*You run too; run home.*)

Then, in English, you tell Jesse to guard his man, and you can tell he's got it. He understands the plan. Now, you just have to get the ball away from Thug 1.

"Hey, aren't you even going to try for a shot?" you question him. "Can you even make a shot?" you challenge.

"Yeah, I can make a shot," he sneers and that's when you get your opportunity.

As soon as he goes for the basket, Fixer Halverson, defensive powerhouse, goes into action. He dribbles once, twice, and on the third one it's yours. Before the Lindonville thugs know what hit them, you and Jesse are running as fast as you can across the court, across the street, and into the woods. You don't even bother to look back.

Go on to the next page.

Once you're a safe distance from them, you slow to a jog and both of you start laughing.

"Oh my gosh," Jesse says breathlessly. "I can't believe that just happened."

"I know," you agree. "That was crazy." Then you add, "How's the arm?"

He rubs it and shrugs. You think he's not letting on how much it really hurts, and you start to worry that maybe it's broken, which would mean hospitals and doctors and definitely getting busted for sneaking out.

This was pretty awesome though, and it might be worth it even if you did get caught.

"We make a good team," Jesse observes, and you agree. You think that no matter what happens with your parents, and no matter how messed up things might get, you and Jesse will handle it just fine together.

THE END

You really appreciate that Jesse is feeling courageous, but if you're going to play two-on-two, you think you'd rather have your trusted teammate and friend, Ashton, to help you. Jesse stares at the ground, disappointed.

"Sorry, bud," you offer, but he just shrugs.

"I need to call my teammate," you tell the Lindonville thugs.

"Fine, whatever," the one guy says, as he pretends to wipe his butt with the ball. These guys are real jerks.

Luckily, Ashton answers right away and he is psyched for a reason to sneak out and play basketball. He says he'll be over in a second, and he is. Ashton comes running up with a huge grin on his face, ready to take these guys out.

Ashton is the second tallest guy on your team, next to you, and although these guys have a couple years and some muscle mass on you two, that's about all they have.

"Okay, guys," you say. "Let's play street ball rules: one game, first to 21."

They agree, and you add, "And when we win, I'm taking my ball and going home."

Ashton laughs at your joke, but the Lindonville thugs laugh because they don't think you'll be taking your ball at all.

You start off with some tight defense, which is no surprise, and you shut them down immediately, blocking lay-ups and dunks, and grabbing rebounds. Ashton is on point and you're playing center.

Go on to the next page.

When it's his ball, he passes to you.

You slice to the rim as soon as you get open. Then those thugs double team you, so Ashton cuts to the hoop and you pass to him for an easy two points.

Since the game is to 21, you don't have to worry about losing your energy, and you are determined to pound these guys, so you play as hard as you can. It's not very long before you're beating them, and they don't like it very much.

Thug 1 keeps yelling at Thug 2, telling him what he's doing wrong.

Ashton sees an opportunity here and starts trash-talking Thug 2, so it's almost like he's ganging up on the guy with his own teammate. It's genius.

You and Ash trounce them and, although they are pretty sore losers, they do give the ball back. You toss it to Jesse, who has been quietly watching from the edge of the court. You hope he isn't too bummed you called Ashton.

"Man, Fixer," Ashton says as the Lindonville thugs walk away, "you brought some serious game tonight."

It felt good to wipe the court with those jerks, but you're not feeling like much of a fixer right now. Maybe on the walk home, you'll be able to smooth things over with Jesse. You hope so.

THE END

Coach wants you to see a counselor, but you're just not sure. Truth is, you just want to play ball and you don't want to think about the mess with your family anymore. Besides, seeing a school counselor sounds too embarrassing.

"I understand," Coach says, putting a hand on your shoulder. "I'm not going to push you, but if you change your mind, just say the word."

"Yes, sir. Thanks."

"And, just so we're clear, this doesn't change my policy about academics," he reminds you.

You say you understand and promise you won't be late again. You also promise you'll focus more on your schoolwork. You hope you can deliver.

The next night, you guys really bring your energy onto the court. Tommy scores twice in the first five minutes; you score right after that. The Dragons' offense is killing it. By midway through the second half, you're up by 14 points, so Coach subs Mark Cunningham for you.

Coach is really great about giving court time to all 12 guys on your team. He believes that in elementary and middle school, it can't just be about winning; it has to be about creating passionate athletes. He says that kids don't join sports teams to sit on the bench and watch their teammates play. When it's a game against the Lions though, stronger players do see a little more time on the floor.

You happen to be sitting on the bench when your mom shows up with Jesse. She looks like she just rolled out of bed, all haggard and

Go on to the next page.

disheveled. She's holding onto your brother as if letting him go would unleash an unspeakable evil on the world. *What did he do now?* A dull ache starts to pulse through your forehead. Unfortunately, this is when Coach decides to send you back in.

You're distracted, and it seems like the other team can sense it. The Lions' offense moves past you like you're not even there. They start scoring like mad and, suddenly, they've got you by only a point with just seconds left. Then, the worst thing happens. You get fouled. Even on a good night, you can't knock down a free throw, and now your mind is somewhere else. You shoot and miss both free throws. The Dragons lose the game.

You're not sure what to do. You're really upset about being distracted by your family, and you don't want to deal with them right now, but you hate to see your mom so unhappy. Should you go home after the game, or go to Ashton's for pizza and strategizing?

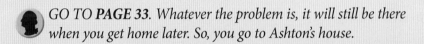 *GO TO **PAGE 33**. Whatever the problem is, it will still be there when you get home later. So, you go to Ashton's house.*

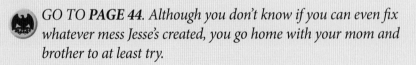 *GO TO **PAGE 44**. Although you don't know if you can even fix whatever mess Jesse's created, you go home with your mom and brother to at least try.*

You can't believe these Lindonville bullies stole your ball and pushed your little brother. Jesse looks a little freaked out, but he's off the court and away from the other guy too, so he seems safe. Besides, you think these guys are just messing around, and you know you've got the skills to get the ball back, even if you simply get it back and run for it.

"Yeah, I could take it," you answer the guy who stole the ball from your brother.

"Well," he says, spinning the ball on his finger. "How about a little one-on-one? Let's see what you've got."

You immediately charge him and make him lose his concentration, but he doesn't drop the ball; he tucks it under his arm like a football and charges back at you.

"Do you even know how to play basketball?" you mock him.

"You don't want to mess with me kid," he warns.

"No," you say. "I don't. I just want my ball back."

They guy practically refuses to dribble, and he hasn't even tried to make a shot. It seems like he's playing keep-away, not basketball.

"C'mon, already," you say. "Are we playing basketball or what?"

He dances around some more like an ape, laughing and holding the ball under his arm.

"Hey," his buddy calls out. "I wanna play too."

"Do you actually want to play?" you ask again.

"Yes, you little party-pooper," he says, scowling at you. "Let's play

Go on to the next page.

two-on-two."

You look at Jesse to see what his face will tell you, because you don't want to put him on the spot and ask him. Plus, even if he is into it, you're not sure Jesse is the best candidate. One of your best friends, who also happens to be an excellent ball player, lives right around the corner. Ashton could easy sneak out and be here in couple of minutes if you called him.

"I could do it," Jesse offers. "Let's get our ball back."

You really appreciate that Jesse has found his courage, and you know he has speed on his side, but his technical skills are lacking. Still, there's more than one way to get that ball back. You're not sure what to do.

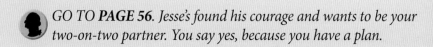 GO TO **PAGE 56**. *Jesse's found his courage and wants to be your two-on-two partner. You say yes, because you have a plan.*

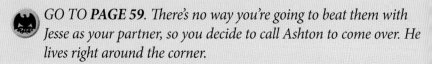 GO TO **PAGE 59**. *There's no way you're going to beat them with Jesse as your partner, so you decide to call Ashton to come over. He lives right around the corner.*